KU-732-957

The Head had asked Axel to come to his office.

"I wonder why the Head needs to see me," Axel thought. He knocked on the door and went inside.

The Head's face was smiling at Axel from the hologram projector on the desk.

"I have something to tell you about the school trip today," the Head said.

The children were going on a trip to Bubba Rand's Rubber Band Factory. They needed some new stretchy material for their super suits.

The Exagger-tron

by Philip Ardagh
Illustrated by Bill Ledger

30131 05646732 4
LONDON BOROUGH OF BARNET

In this story ...

Axel
(Invisiboy)

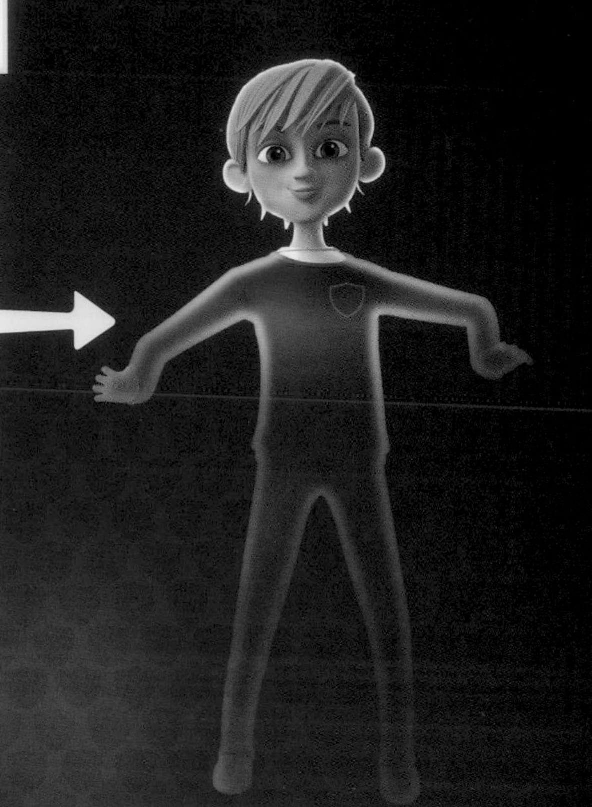

Axel has the power to turn invisible. This is very useful for sneaking up on baddies. It's also handy when playing hide-and-seek with friends.

Magnus
(caretaker)

The Head
(head teacher)

"I'm afraid you're not going, Axel," the Head said. "I have a special task for you instead. Please go and see Magnus at once. You have permission to enter Corridor B12."

"Cool!" Axel thought. Pupils were not normally allowed in Corridor B12.

"What could the task be?" Axel wondered.

Axel soon found Magnus standing by a huge armour-plated door. It was held shut by a chunky padlock.

"Why don't you open it?" said Magnus, handing Axel the key.

Axel trembled with excitement. He turned the key and pulled the door open, wondering what incredible adventures lay ahead.

Axel's heart sank. It was a room full of dust-covered junk.

"I was expecting something more … well, impressive," he said. "What is this place?"

“It’s the gadget storeroom,” the caretaker explained. “It’s where the academy stores all the gadgets that have been taken from villains. Very few people are allowed in here.”

"Then why are we here?" Axel asked.

"The energy-drain field has broken," replied Magnus.

"The what?" said Axel.

"The energy-drain field. It stops the villains' gadgets from working," explained Magnus. "We have to repair it, or the gadgets will cause havoc!"

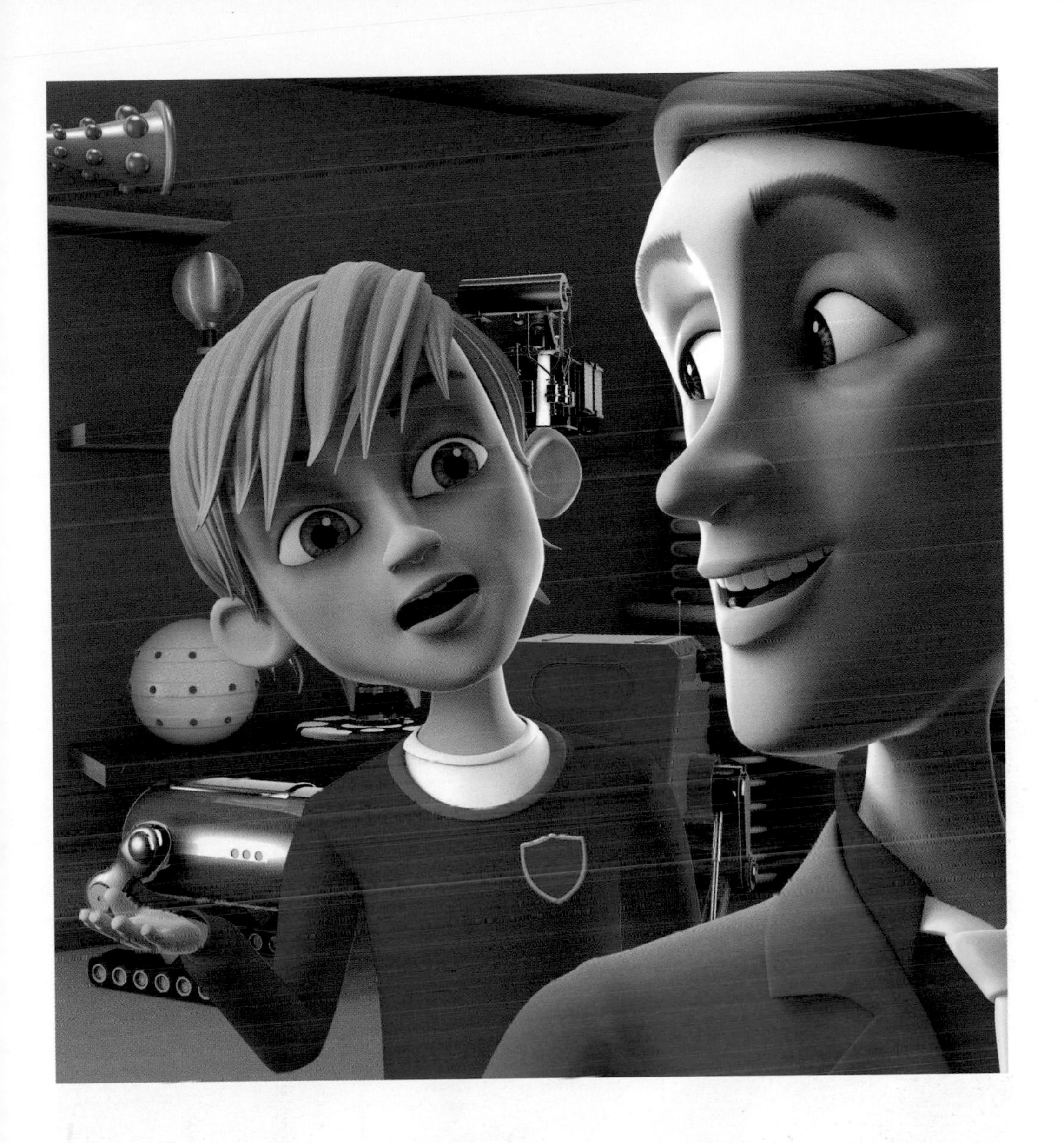

"But I have no idea how to repair an energy-drain field," said Axel.

"I know how to fix it," said Magnus. "Your job is to hand me the right tools."

Axel sighed. He wished he had gone to the rubber band factory instead. He picked up the nearest gadget. It was lime green, looked like a camera but had a large, silver cog in the middle.

Magnus looked up in alarm. "DON'T TOUCH THAT!" he shouted.

Axel was so shocked, he dropped the gadget. It hit the floor and began to make a strange humming noise, like a swarm of tone-deaf wasps. Then a beam of red light shot out and hit Axel.

"W-what's happening?" gasped Axel. His whole body tingled. He was beginning to disappear! He could usually disappear and reappear whenever he wanted … but not this time. No, this time he couldn't reappear however hard he tried!

Another beam of red light shot out and hit Magnus. He immediately started behaving strangely. He rushed out of the storeroom and ran down the corridor at high speed. He was searching his pockets and shouting: "I'm sure I've got one somewhere!" and "I'll fix it!"

Axel watched the caretaker go. He snatched up the lime-green gadget again. On the back were the words: Ranter Enterprises.

Axel spotted a computer on a nearby desk. He wiped the dust from the screen, switched it on and went to the Super Villains page. When he typed 'Ranter' in the search box, a single entry appeared.

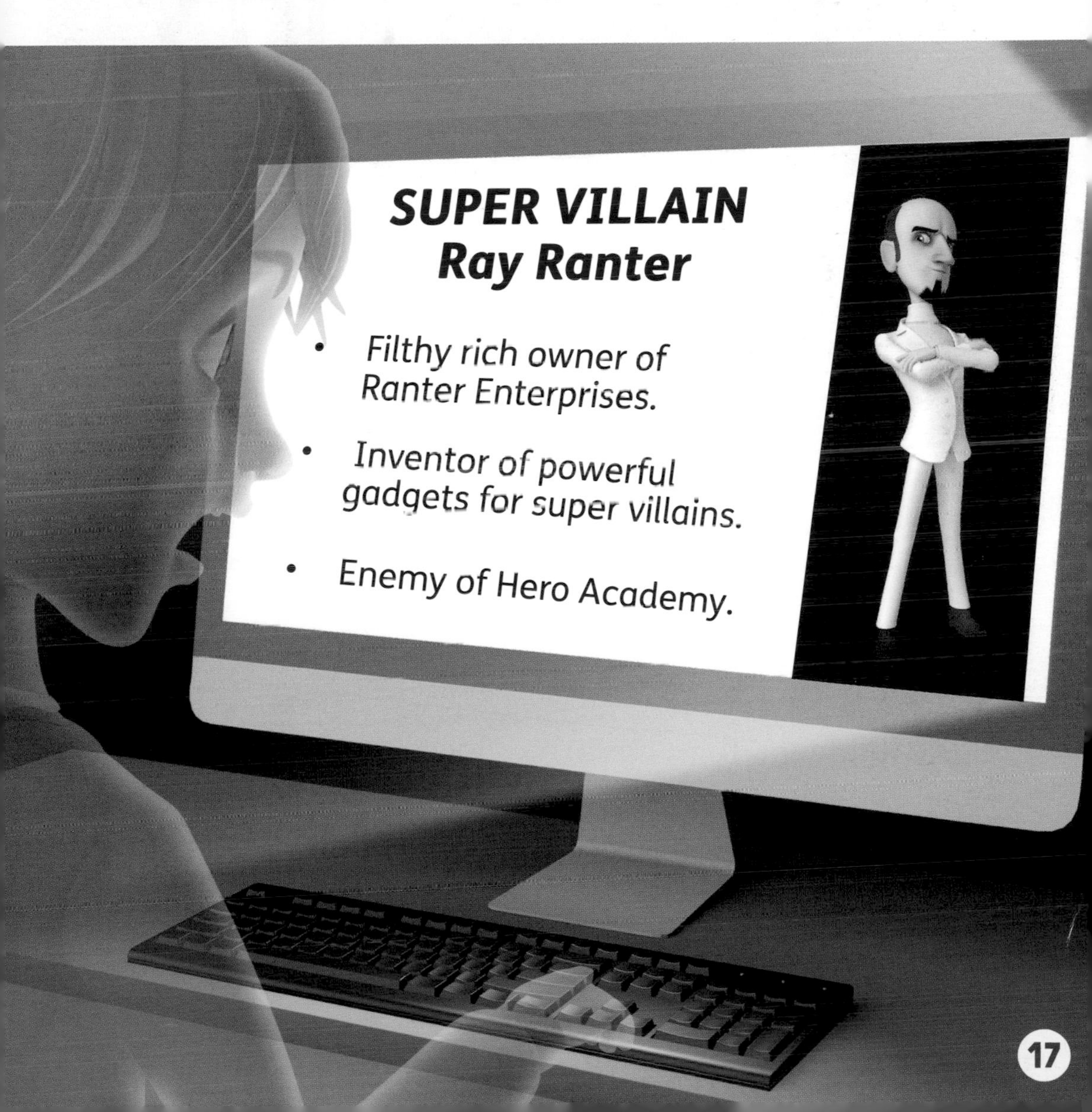

Axel tapped a few more computer keys. An article appeared from ten years ago.

HERO ACADEMY WEEKLY BULLETIN

New gadget storeroom opened!

Hero Academy has opened a storeroom for all the gadgets that have been taken away from super villains. The first gadget locked away was made by Ray Ranter. The Exagger-tron 350 can exaggerate superpowers and make people's behaviour hard to control.

"So that's it!" said Axel. "The Exagger-tron 350 is stopping me from controlling my invisibility ... and it's also making Magnus do all his jobs at once!"

At that moment, Magnus charged in, shouting, "Busy! Busy! Busy!"

Axel looked down at the gadget. He looked at the silver cog in the middle. There was only one thing for it. He turned the dial the other way and pressed the button. This time, there was a high-pitched whistle, a green beam shot out …

… and Axel began to reappear.

Phew! It worked.

Axel ran down the empty corridor and found Magnus. He was painting a wall and sweeping the floor at the same time. Axel pressed the button and another green beam shot out from the gadget. Magnus was soon back to his old, slower self.

By the time Axel's classmates returned, Magnus had repaired the energy-drain field (with Axel helpfully passing him the right tools).

"We need to make sure the Exagger-tron 350 doesn't cause any more problems," Magnus said.

Axel wrapped the Exagger-tron 350 in old newspaper, then put it in a thick envelope. He then wrapped it in more newspaper and then tin foil. Magnus found just the thing to hold it all together ... some of Bubba Rand's rubber bands!